BAGELS COME HOME!

Joan Betty Stuchner

illustrations by Dave Whamond

D1509689

ORCA BOOK PUBLISHERS

Text copyright © 2014 Joan Betty Stuchner
Illustrations copyright © 2014 Dave Whamond

All rights reserved. No part of this publication may be reproduced or transmitted in
any form or by any means, electronic or mechanical, including photocopying,
recording or by any information storage and retrieval system now known or to be
invented, without permission in writing from the publisher.

Library and Archives Canada Cataloguing in Publication

Stuchner, Joan Betty, author
Bagels come home / Joan Betty Stuchner ;
illustrated by Dave Whamond.
(Orca echoes)

Issued in print and electronic formats.
ISBN 978-1-4598-0346-6 (pbk.).--ISBN 978-1-4598-0347-3 (pdf).
ISBN 978-1-4598-0348-0 (epub)

1. Dogs--Juvenile fiction. I. Whamond, Dave, illustrator
II. Title. III. Series: Orca echoes
PS8587.T825B33 2014   jc813'.54   c2013-906853-8
c2013-906854-6

First published in the United States, 2014
Library of Congress Control Number: 2013955773

Summary: Josh learns just how much work a puppy can be when he adopts Bagels.

Orca Book Publishers gratefully acknowledges the support for its publishing programs
provided by the following agencies: the Government of Canada through the Canada Book Fund
and the Canada Council for the Arts, and the Province of British Columbia
through the BC Arts Council and the Book Publishing Tax Credit.

MIX
Paper from
responsible sources
FSC **FSC® C004071**
www.fsc.org

*Orca Book Publishers is dedicated to preserving the environment and
has printed this book on Forest Stewardship Council® certified paper.*

Cover artwork and interior illustrations by Dave Whamond
Author photo by Tom Kavadias

ORCA BOOK PUBLISHERS   ORCA BOOK PUBLISHERS
PO Box 5626, STN. B   PO Box 468
Victoria, BC Canada   Custer, WA USA
V8R 6S4   98240-0468

www.orcabook.com
Printed and bound in Canada.

17 16 15 14 • 4 3 2 1

For Pam and Dave Mason—hosts with the
most—who seem to prefer sharks to dogs.
Another story for another time.
And for Tom and Dov, as always.

CHAPTER ONE
I (Josh Bernstein) Want A Dog

There's this old movie on television called *Lassie Come Home*. That's how I get the idea for us to buy a dog. We have a goldfish (Lox) and a cat (Creamcheese). It only makes sense to get a dog. Right? My little sister Becky likes the idea.

Even my parents are on board.

Mom says, "Good idea, Josh." *Sniff, sniff.* She's crying and smiling at the same time. *Lassie Come Home* is one of those happy/sad movies. After the kid actor, Roddy McDowall, says his line "You're my Lassie come home," Mom blows her nose into one of Dad's big handkerchiefs.

"But we'll get a dog from the shelter. It's a good deed to rescue a dog."

Dad agrees. "Josh is almost nine. That's a good age to get a dog."

"I'm five," says Becky. "That's a good age too."

"Yes, it is," says Mom.

Becky wants to help me take care of the dog. I'm not so sure she'll be much help. I'm the one who changes the water in Lox's bowl (when I remember). Becky tried to help me once. She pulled the plug in the sink too soon. Lox nearly went down the drain.

I'm also the one who cleans out Creamcheese's litter box (maybe not as often as I should). When Becky helped me, she spilled litter all over the carpet. Becky's not a big help. But Dad insists.

"You and Becky can walk the dog together and take care of it. Do we have a deal?"

Do I have a choice? "Deal," I say.

"Deal," says Becky. I love my sister, but…

CHAPTER TWO
The Marpole Shelter for Otherwise Doomed Dogs and Puppies

That's not really its name. It's just called the Marpole Dog Shelter. But we all know what happens to dogs that don't get picked.

A lady in a lab coat, Ms. Pringle, takes us inside to the kennels. I've never seen so many dogs in one place.

Becky stops in front of one big cage and points. "I want that one!"

Ms. Pringle says, "That is a Great Dane/dalmatian cross."

I think it looks like a small pony. Becky's thinking the same thing. She says, "I could put a saddle on him. I could ride him to kindergarten. I could tie him up to a tree and feed him hay at snack time. I could—"

"No," says Dad. "You could *not*."

All the dogs are mixtures. There's a cockapoo (cocker spaniel/poodle), a pugapoo (pug/poodle) and a Yorkipoo (Yorkshire terrier/poodle). There's also a German shepherd/corgi. Big mistake on short legs.

Then we stop outside the last cage and stare.

"That," says Ms. Pringle, "is a whippet/Jack Russell/sheltie mix. He's just a puppy."

This one is different. The other dogs are just hanging around, killing time. This puppy turns cartwheels and does backflips. He runs around the cage.

Dad says, "If there was a canine version of Cirque du Soleil, this dog would be the star turn." Even though Dad has doubts, the rest of us like him. Mom says he has personality.

Dad sighs. "We'll take this one," he says.

He won't admit it, but I think Dad secretly likes our new puppy. After all, he'll fit right in.

We're a pretty theatrical family. Except for me, that is. Mom and Dad act in community theater. Becky would like to, but she's too young.

We're in the car when Mom asks, "What shall we call him?

"Bagels," I say.

Becky frowns. "Why not Bagel?" she asks. "There's only one of him."

"It just sounds better," I tell her.

On the way home, Bagels's travel cage sits between Becky and me. The cage bounces on the seat for the entire trip. I think Bagels is doing an Irish jig. And he howls! Becky stuffs her fingers in her ears. Dad says he thinks Bagels is something called *hyperactive*. You don't need to be Sherlock Holmes to figure that one out. Maybe that's why I like Bagels so much. He's like me. At school my teacher calls me Mr. Fidget.

Mom explains, "Whippets are racing dogs. Jack Russells hunt rats. Shelties are sheep dogs. He's bound to be restless. He'll go to puppy school. That should do the trick."

I've never noticed the calming effect of school. Maybe dog school is different.

CHAPTER THREE
Pets' Paradise

Halfway to our house, we stop at the mini-mall. Mom goes into Pets' Paradise while the rest of us stay in the car. Bagels is still dancing and singing. Dad switches on the radio. It's Rock 101. For a few moments, Bagels is quiet. Then the Irish jig becomes wilder. The singing—if that's what it is—gets louder.

"He likes rock 'n' roll," says Becky.

"All right!" says Dad. "My kind of dog."

See? I was right. Dad *does* like Bagels.

Of course, they're playing, "You Ain't Nothin' but a Hound Dog."

Mom finally comes out of Pets' Paradise. She's pushing a trolley.

Dad sighs. "Looks as if your mother bought enough pet supplies for six puppies."

Mom puts everything in the trunk. She wheels the trolley back and gets in the car.

"Let me guess," says Dad. "There was a sale on at the pet store."

"As a matter of fact," says Mom, "there was. I picked up a few boxes of fish food for Lox and some cans of *Cat Banquet* for Creamcheese. Is that okay?"

"Absolutely!" Dad says. He only argues with Mom when it's really necessary. I guess today it isn't necessary.

We are finally on our way home. Bagels is singing and dancing to "Jailhouse Rock."

"Werooo, werooo, yip, yip." *Kachung*, bounce, *kachung*, bounce.

CHAPTER FOUR
Bagels, Lox and Creamcheese

When we get home, I check the kitchen for Creamcheese, but she's not in her basket. Lox's bowl is on the kitchen shelf. He's swimming round and round. His bowl is full of interesting stuff—a castle, a bridge, a mermaid and tons of greenery.

Bagels doesn't stop yowling. Lox stops in his tracks. Mom lets Bagels out of the carry cage. I swear Lox looks through his bowl and his eyes almost pop out of his head.

Bagels takes off and does circuits around the kitchen. We all jump out of the way.

"Don't worry," says Mom as Bagels skitters by. "Like I said, puppy school will do wonders."

After about ten more circuits, Bagels flops into Creamcheese's basket and falls into a deep sleep.

That's Creamcheese's cue to walk into the kitchen. Her tail's up. She's angry.

Creamcheese is a fat, fluffy, part Persian. Her fur is the color of cream cheese. Creamcheese frowns at Bagels.

Then she hisses. I think she's saying, "Who is sleeping in *my* bed?" Or she could be saying something ruder. Mom scoops her up.

"Creamcheese will be sleeping with us tonight," she tells Dad. Dad doesn't look pleased. Creamcheese doesn't either.

"Bagels might want a midnight snack," says Mom.

She dips into one of the shopping bags. She hands Becky two new bowls. I add the food. Becky pours the water—without spilling much.

Mom had picked up a fluffy dog toy at Pets' Paradise. I put it in the basket next to Bagels. If he wakes up in the night, he won't feel lonely. I watch

him sleep. He's kind of cute. He twitches a lot in his sleep. Mom says Becky and I do that too. Becky giggles. I don't.

Dad and I put newspapers all over the kitchen floor in case Bagels needs to go to the bathroom in the night.

I tell Becky, "You can help me clean up the mess in the morning. Puppy poop isn't so bad." Becky's lips tremble. I know it's a fake tremble. I've seen her practice in the mirror.

We leave the kitchen. I close the door just like I always do. It's my job to close doors and windows at night. Once in a while, I forget. "I'm only eight!" I keep reminding my parents. I sometimes think they don't believe me.

CHAPTER FIVE
Bagels (aka Houdini)

My bedroom is right over the kitchen. That night I dream that a bunch of wild animals have torn the kitchen apart.

In the morning I wake up all sweaty. I listen. Everything is quiet.

I'm first downstairs. Right away I know something's wrong. Mom keeps the laundry basket in the laundry room down the hall from the kitchen. The laundry room door is always closed. I should know. I'm the one who has to close it. But it's wide open. That's impossible. I *remember* closing it.

The basket's been tipped over and it's...empty! Laundry is scattered all over the floor leading up to the kitchen.

I don't have to open the kitchen door. It's already open. My nightmare is real! The kitchen looks as if it's been torn apart by stampeding bison. Bagels's fluffy dog toy has been ripped open. Its guts are scattered everywhere.

Bagels is standing on top of the kitchen table. There's a pair of Dad's tartan boxer shorts on his head and a bagel in his mouth.

"Well," I say to him, "I guess I gave you the right name."

But how did he get into the bagel bag? Mom keeps it on top of the fridge. The bag is now on the floor in front of the fridge. It's empty. Chewed-up bagels are everywhere. And other stuff. Lucky we spread newspapers all over the floor.

I don't see Becky behind me. But I hear her.

"Josh, do we have to clean up this mess?"

"I think so, Becky."

"I guess we don't have any bagels for breakfast."

"Nope."

When Mom and Dad come downstairs, they just stare at the mess. Dad looks at Bagels. Then he looks at me.

"Josh, did you remember to close the doors?"

"Yes," I tell him. "I swear I did."

At first he just says, "You *think* you did."

But then he looks at Bagels again. He thinks for a second or two. "Maybe we should change his name to Houdini," he says. "I mean, if you're right about closing the doors. Houdini was a famous escape artist. You never know, Bagels might be one too."

That's when I notice Creamcheese. She's sitting in her basket. How did she get here? She's supposed to be in Mom and Dad's room. She looks around. Her lip is curled in a sneer. Or whatever cats have instead of lips. Then she stands, flips her fat, fluffy tail and walks out of the room. I just know she's up to something.

I glance at Lox in the fish bowl. The water's so cloudy, I can barely see him. Maybe it's time for me to clean it out.

In two weeks Bagels will go to puppy school. I can't wait to see his first report card. But right now I have to change the water in Lox's bowl. Next, Becky and I have to help clean up Bagels's mess. Then we have to take Bagels for a walk. Mom's coming too.

"Don't forget to take some plastic bags," Dad says. "In case Bagels needs to go to the bathroom."

I tell Mom, "He's already been to the bathroom. Or should I say, the kitchen." I grab some plastic bags anyway.

CHAPTER SIX
A Run in the Park

I look up Houdini in a book about famous people. He's this guy from about a hundred years ago. His job was to escape from chains and from locked-up trunks. Sounds like Bagels.

Bagels escapes a few more times before our first big family outing. One time, he gets out of a window that Dad swears he locked. When we search the neighborhood, we don't see him right away. We hear him though.

"Werooo! Werooo!" Two blocks from our house, Bagels has rounded up some joggers. They're pretty upset by the time Mom and I arrive on the scene. Mom just smiles and tells them it's the sheltie part of him.

"They can't help themselves. It's in the blood. They usually round up sheep." The joggers aren't interested in Bagels's family history.

One jogger uses a word I've never heard before. Mom won't tell me what it means.

When we get back home, Creamcheese is stretched out on the sill. The window is half open. She looks at me and smiles as if she has a secret. Honest. I don't make these things up. Her paw is on the bar that's part of the window latch. Dad goes to close the window and Creamcheese begins to lick her paw. She's wearing this innocent look that cats wear when they're up to no good.

Another time, I'm taking Bagels for a short walk around the block. His collar isn't that loose, but when I'm not looking, he slips through it and races down the street. Then he leaps into Mr. Sparkman's fish pond. The fish all have heart attacks and die. Mr. Sparkman shakes his fist as I drag a wet Bagels out of the pond.

"Those were my prize koi," he shouts.

I tell him he could always make them into gefilte fish.[1] He gets even angrier. Maybe I'm thinking of a different kind of fish.

Mom decides we should take Bagels out more.

"We'll have a family outing in the park. That way Bagels will get tired out. He won't need to escape. He's just restless."

The park's almost empty. There's only a German shepherd running around after a ball. The dog's owner is sitting on a bench. He doesn't even stand up once. Every time the dog brings back the ball, the man just throws the ball farther than before. Then he shouts, "Bruno, go get it."

"People like that shouldn't have dogs," Mom growls.

As soon as Bagels sees that ball, his ears and tail perk up. I *swear* I'm holding the leash real tight. But it doesn't matter. Bagels jerks it out of my hand

---

[1] Gefilte Fish is a Jewish dish using whitefish mixed up with other ingredients. Not to be made with fish from your neighbor's pond.

and does a double somersault before running straight for the ball.

Bagels reaches the ball just ahead of Bruno. Bruno is angry. He bares his teeth at Bagels, but Bagels laughs in the face of danger. He shakes the ball in Bruno's face. He dances a jig. He runs away at top speed. Bruno chases him.

Bruno's owner shouts, "Bruno!"

Bruno seems to be deaf. He runs after Bagels as if his life depends on it. Finally, the man gets up from the bench.

"Bruno! Here! Now!" Maybe Bruno needs a hearing aid, like my grandma.

"Bagels!" I yell. "Heel!" I've heard people say that to dogs.

Bagels ignores me. If he knows what *heel* means, he's not letting on.

Besides, I figure the whippet in Bagels has taken over.

They do four laps around the park, and Bruno doesn't have a chance. After the fourth lap he collapses

in a heap. He just lays there panting with his tongue hanging out. His eyes are rolling around in his head like a dog in a TV cartoon.

While his owner runs to Bruno's aid, Bagels does a victory lap. He drops the ball as he passes Bruno, then runs up to me. He grins and dances that jig. He lets me pick up the leash and we all walk home. The strange thing is that now when I say "heel," he seems to know exactly what it means. From now on, I'm going to hold extra tight to that leash.

Bagels doesn't stop escaping from the house, but he always gets hungry and comes home. I can't help noticing that each time Bagels goes missing, Creamcheese is standing by an open window.

I tell myself I'm imagining things. And yet…

"So that we can all sleep in peace," Mom says, "I've finally put a latch on the laundry room door." She puts another on the kitchen door.

She says, "Of course, once Bagels has been to school, we won't have to worry anymore."

CHAPTER SEVEN
School Days

Bagels's first day of school finally arrives. It's at the community center. Dad decides I should be the one to train Bagels. I don't mind. He's become the brother I never had. Becky wants to train Bagels too. I tell her I'll show her everything the instructor shows me.

"Promise?"

"I promise."

There are three classes: Beginner Basics, Beginner Socialization and Advanced Obedience. We're in the Beginner Basics. It teaches dogs to obey simple commands like "sit," "stay" and "heel." It doesn't include "don't leave the house without permission" or "don't jump in the neighbor's pond." I'm guessing that's Advanced Obedience.

Mom decides to come along with Becky. "Just to watch." They sit on a bench at the back.

The room is full of puppies on leashes. We all stand in a circle and say our names and our dogs' names. Most of the puppies are restless and jiggly. So am I. I force myself to keep still. I'm okay if no one tells me to keep still. It's only when I have to be still that I have trouble. Puppies have the same problem.

Even after fifteen minutes, a few puppies can't keep still. Some walk around their owners' legs. Leashes are getting tangled. The teacher barks a few commands. We all pull on the leashes, and most of the puppies become calmer. Except for Bagels.

Bagels is doing his usual backflips and the occasional Irish jig. The teacher walks up to us. She frowns at Bagels and wags her finger at him. She says he'll have to spend some time in the "Naughty Corner" if he doesn't behave.

Bagels is really interested in the instructor's finger. His head moves in time with it as if he's being hypnotized by a magician who is waving a shiny watch and saying, "You are feeling very sleepy."

Something tells me Bagels is *not* feeling sleepy.

"Naughty Bagels," the instructor says. "Very naughty. Sit still. Still." That's when Bagels jumps up and bites the teacher's finger. Not very hard. I mean, there's only a drop or two of blood. Three at the most. The teacher yelps.

"Naughty, naughty Bagels!" the teacher says again. She turns to me. "Bagels is *not* ready for school," she tells me.

Bagels pees on her leg.

We are told to leave.

Sometimes life doesn't seem fair.

Out on the street, Becky says, "I don't like that lady."

Mom says, "She didn't seem very patient."

When we get home, Becky says, "Maybe if I bite my teacher's finger I could get kicked out of kindergarten."

Mom says she doesn't think that's a good idea.

Dad's not happy. "If Bagels can't be trained, we might have to send him back."

"Noooo!" says Becky. "He'll learn, Dad. Honest. Just like we did. We got trained. Right, Josh?"

I say, "Becky's right, Dad. Bagels will learn."

Later on, I'm in my room trying to get Bagels to sit. He just runs around after his tail. Becky comes in.

"Bagels won't have to go back to the kennel, will he?"

"No, Becky," I say. Except I'm not so sure.

"If we don't behave, will they send *us* back?"

I look at Becky. She's close to tears.

"Back where?" I ask.

"Where we came from," she says. "The kids' kennel."

"We didn't come from a kids' kennel, Becky."

"Oh."

But now I'm worried. I read somewhere about boarding schools. Maybe they'd send us to one.

It's not like real school, where you go home every day. You actually live there. I hear they make you have cold showers and eat lumpy porridge for breakfast. On the other hand, a boarding school is probably expensive. My parents don't have enough money. That's a relief.

Besides, I'm determined that Bagels and I will be the best-behaved puppy-and-boy team ever.

CHAPTER EIGHT
Back to School

The dog instructor agrees to give Bagels another chance. A week later we take him back to class. I've managed to teach him how to sit. Sometimes. When he feels like it. But he still escapes. We can't figure out how.

"No one ever figured out Houdini's secret either," says Dad.

"I have high hopes," Mom tells me as we walk into the community center. *My* hopes are very low.

When we walk into the class, I know it's a mistake. You know how at school there's always a kid who stirs things up? All the kids are trying hard to behave except this one kid? Mom says her sister, my aunt Sharon, was that kid.

"Put your aunt Sharon in a room full of angels and they'd be devils by recess."

I guess the other kids think, if this one can break the rules, why can't I?

Bagels is like Aunt Sharon.

Bagels and I get into the circle, and all the other pups want to run up and say hi. While their owners yank on the leashes, Bagels barks "Hi!" to each of his long-lost friends.

The instructor glares at Bagels and says, "Now, puppies, let's not forget our manners. Let's show Bagels Bernstein what we've all been learning, shall we?"

Bagels is the only dog who refuses to walk to heel. He wants to play with his friends. The instructor walks over to me.

"Josh, here's a trick that might help. When the dog pulls on its leash, stand still. Then rein him in a little. He will back up until he reaches your side. It never fails."

I try. It fails. Instead of backing up, Bagels runs around me three times and trips me up. I fall flat on my face. It hurts. Bagels tries to lick it better.

The instructor sends us home and says she'll give us one more chance. "Come back next week. He might have settled down by then," she says.

But she doesn't say it like she means it.

I'll keep this pretty short. Bagels's third time at puppy school doesn't last very long. When we walk into class, Bagels is happy to see his old friends. So happy that he yanks the leash out of my hands and flies across the room. The other puppies do the same thing. In seconds all the leashes are braided together. It looks as if the puppies are in the middle of a Maypole dance around one of the chairs.

At the end of five minutes, one of the pups—a poodle, I think—has peed on the floor.

The dachshund has pooped, and Bagels—trust me, you don't really want to know what Bagels does. But I have to clean it up.

I can't be sure, but I think the instructor says, "Never darken our doors again."

CHAPTER NINE
Peter Pan

A few weeks after Bagels is finally expelled from school, he's doing pretty good. He's close to being toilet trained. He almost always walks to heel. He sits when commanded (unless something catches his eye, like a squirrel climbing up a tree). He still escapes now and then, but as Mom says, "You can't have everything."

It's lucky that Bagels is behaving well, because Mom and Dad have other things on their minds. Like *Peter Pan.*

My parents belong to a theater group called the Marpole Players. This year they're starring in *Peter Pan.* They've rehearsed for weeks and weeks, even though there are only two performances.

Usually, Becky and I see the shows with Aunt Sharon. This year there are two last-minute emergencies. First of all, Aunt Sharon has to have her tonsils out. Second of all, the guy doing props for the show has the flu. My parents decide I can handle the job. I know I'm only eight (almost nine), but I've been backstage a lot. I know how things work. Becky has to sit backstage near me so I can watch her.

Becky's excited to be this close to the stage. Her eyes are shining. I tell her, "I'll let you give props to the actors. But you have to listen to me. Okay?"

"Sure."

She's gazing around. I don't think she's really listening to me.

Backstage is fine with me. You'll never get me out on a stage. Becky, on the other hand, can't wait to be onstage. Mom and Dad say she's too young right now.

"Can't I be a Lost Boy? I don't even need lines."

"Maybe next year," says Mom.

I look up. As well as doing props, I have to help one of the stagehands pull on the ropes that open the curtains.

The ropes reach way up, almost to the ceiling. There are lights and wires up there too.

Dad tells me, "It's an important job. I know you can do it, Josh. Just do whatever Naomi tells you to do." Naomi is the stage manager.

The props table already has stuff on it. Most of the actors just grab what they need before they go onstage. For instance, Captain Hook needs his fake sword. Peter Pan needs his fake dagger. John needs his umbrella. I have to make sure they all take the right prop.

Captain Hook/Mr. Darling (my dad) tells me, "When the actors walk offstage, you make sure they return their props."

Mrs. Darling (my mom) says, "Keep an eye on Becky, please." Becky's not happy. All she can think about is being one of the Lost Boys. Mom still says,

"No, and that's final," so Becky sits down near the props table and pouts.

"Places, everyone!" shouts Naomi.

"Break a leg," says Mom to Dad.

"*Merde*," says Dad to Mom.

"What's that mean?" asks Becky.

"I think it's French for 'break a leg,'" I tell her. "Hush. The show's about to start."

CHAPTER TEN
Flying Bagels

You're probably asking yourself, "Where's Bagels?" Well, the answer is he's at home with Creamcheese and Lox. Dad went around the house twice to make sure every window and door was completely Bagels-proof.

"I'll say it again," he said. "We should have called that dog Houdini."

The show's about to begin. Backstage we can hear the sounds of people entering the auditorium. When everyone has sat down, the lights dim. Everything's quiet. I have to admit, that part's exciting. I'm stage left. The stagehand on stage right gives me a nod. Then he and I open the curtains. Becky helps me pull the rope. At least, Becky *thinks* that she's helping.

The actors are in place.

Becky's perched on her chair, close to me so she can see the show. Everything's fine until I hear, "Weroof! Weroof!"

A bark is like a fingerprint. No two are alike. And I'd know that bark anywhere.

"It's Bagels," whispers Becky. She smiles.

"No kidding," I say. I'm not smiling.

"How'd he get here?" Becky asks.

"He's an escape artist, that's how," I tell her.

Then Bagels is doing laps around me and panting. They say dogs have a good sense of smell. I guess I smell pretty strong. He figured out where to find me—three blocks away from our house.

I grab Bagels's collar. He stops doing laps and jumps up to lick my face. I love him, but the show must go on.

"Becky," I whisper, "find a rope or something strong. We have to tie him up until the show's over."

Becky says, "But I'm not supposed to move. Mom and Dad said so."

"Becky," I say, "it's an emergency. Mom and Dad would understand. I give you permission to get off the chair and help me. Like right now!"

She slides off the chair and looks around.

"How about this?" she says. She's found a dog harness on the props table.

Wait a minute. What's a dog harness doing on the props table? Nana doesn't wear one. It must be a mistake. I pick it up and fasten it to Bagels' body.

He tries to wriggle out of it. But I have to make sure Bagels doesn't spoil the show. I need something to tie him to.

That's when I see the wire hanging nearby. It's close to the fake window that leads to the stage. It has a clip attached to it. I guess it's for an overhead light or something. I hook the harness onto the clip. I tell Bagels, "Don't move until the show is over."

He looks offended. "Wrup, wrup, weroof," he says.

"Don't argue," I say.

A second later, Peter Pan rushes up to me. He checks the props table. His face goes blank. "The harness? Where's the harness?"

"It's okay," I say. "I put it around Bagels."

Peter Pan looks confused. "Bagels?" he says. "You put my harness around some bread rolls?"

I shake my head. "My dog. He's called Bagels."

Naomi appears. "What's the holdup?" she asks. Without waiting for an answer, she waves to the stagehand on stage right. He pulls on a rope or lever with one hand and picks up a book with the other. Bagels gives a yip and shoots up into the air, flying through the fake window. He looks pretty surprised.

"What the...?" says Naomi.

We all watch Bagels fly from the wings to above center stage.

Peter Pan's jaw drops. Naomi says a bad word.

At first the audience is very quiet. Bagels grins.

"That's supposed to be me up there," hisses Peter Pan.

Suddenly there's a lot of noise.

"What's that?" I ask.

Becky looks upset. "It's the audience. People are laughing at Bagels."

But then there's another noise. Applause. People are clapping. Bagels barks. He likes it. Becky's not upset anymore. She grins at me. Mom and Dad (the Darlings) are standing in the wings on upstage right. They look dazed.

Onstage, the Darling children are sitting on their beds. Wendy, Michael and John stare up at Bagels in silence. Finally, Peter Pan decides to go onstage without a harness. He climbs through the fake window and leaps around the room as if he's flying. No one notices. They're all looking at Bagels.

The stagehand on stage right still hasn't noticed anything. He's reading his book. As he pulls the wire, Bagels flies all around the stage. The stagehand must have done this a lot at rehearsal. He thinks he doesn't need to look.

Becky and I watch as Bagels goes around and around. It's what Bagels does best. Only he's usually running in circles. This is his first time flying.

That's when Nana sees what's going on. Nana is an enormous Old English sheepdog. She's wearing a lacy cap and a matching apron that's tied on with strings and Velcro. She rushes in from upstage right, followed by the dresser, who's been trying to remove Nana's leash. Nana leaps into the air, howling.

"Wowowowowow!"

She's trying to bite Bagel's dangling tail. The dresser is trying to stop her.

"Down, down. Stop!" says the dresser.

But Nana doesn't stop. She runs around the stage, looking up at Bagels while the dresser tries to grab the leash.

Each time Bagels spins around the set, the crowd cheers. The audience is having fun. So is Bagels.

When the dresser chases Nana over the beds and back again, the applause is deafening. Wendy, Michael and John

run for cover. They sit on the windowsill. Nana and the dresser knock over a couple of lamps and a rocking chair.

Bagels is lowered to a bedpost, then a bureau, but not for long. Soon he's back flying through the air.

The stage manager puts her head in her hands. "The director's in the front row," she says. "He'll run me out of town for this. It's the end of my theatrical career."

I try to comfort her. "It's only community theater."

She glares at me. "Some of the world's greatest stage managers had their start in community theater."

"What about Bagels?" Becky says. "It's probably the end of his career too."

I'm thinking the same thing. Except that Bagels is having a great time. At home, we're always telling him not to do this kind of stuff. Here, there are three hundred people shouting, "More, more!"

"Listen," I tell Becky. "They like him!"

"Of course they do," says Becky. "He's a great actor."

"I hope Mom and Dad aren't angry," I say.

Becky can't hear me. The applause is too loud.

CHAPTER ELEVEN
A Star is Born

Mom/Mrs. Darling is wagging her finger at Bagels. "Bad dog, Bagels. You spoiled the show. Peter Pan is very angry."

She doesn't mention that Wendy, Michael and John are in their dressing rooms crying hysterically. She doesn't have to. I can hear them.

Dad says, "It probably wasn't a good idea to get a dog."

I'm just about to defend Bagels when the director rushes backstage.

"Do you hear the applause? I've never had such a successful show!" He looks at me. "I understand that's your dog." He points at Bagels. "You sure trained him to be a star! Would it be okay if…"

"Bagels," I say with pride.

"Right," he says. "Bagels. Can he come back tomorrow for the second show?"

Mom and Dad look at each other. Becky and I look at each other. The director promises, "He can have top billing."

"Weroof!" says Bagels.

Bagels is allowed to fly for the rest of the show. He steals every scene. The audience especially likes the one where Bagels joins Captain Hook and the Crocodile.

At the end of the show, Bagels takes three curtain calls.

"We'd better get home," says Mom. "Bagels ought to get a good night's sleep if he's performing tomorrow night."

CHAPTER TWELVE
"Starring Bagels Bernstein"

It actually says that on the new poster.

I get to be props person again. I don't mess up even once.

Becky has managed to talk Mom and Dad into letting her be a Lost Boy. "A *silent* Lost Boy," Mom insists.

The show goes without a hitch. Bagels gets four curtain calls *and* a standing ovation. He loves it! The rest of the cast don't seem to mind. Bagels has won them over.

When it's time to go home, Dad turns to me. "Josh," he says, "you and Becky made us proud."

"Weroof," says Bagels.

Mom pats Bagels. "You too, Bagels. You made us proud."

We're driving home from Bagels's closing-night success. Becky, Bagels and I are in the backseat. Becky whispers something to me. "I should have told you this before," she says. "Don't tell Mom and Dad. They might get rid of Creamcheese. After all, she isn't a star like Bagels."

"What is it?" I ask.

That's when she tells me what I've suspected all along.

"I've seen Creamcheese practicing how to open doors and windows. She's really good at it. It sounds crazy, Josh, but I think she's been getting Bagels into trouble."

"Not so crazy, Becky," I say. "From now on, we're going to have to keep an eye on those two."

She looks at me, eyes wide. "Me too?"

"You too," I tell her. "Tonight you were a great Lost Boy."

"Really?"

"Really." And I mean it. "Two stars were born tonight, Becky."

She beams like a flashlight.

"Thanks, Josh."

"Don't mention it, sis."

Bagels the showstopper is fast asleep on my knee.

I put my chin on his head and whisper something from one of the great movie classics. "You're my Bagels come home."

JOAN BETTY STUCHNER has never actually owned a dog, but she's known quite a few, including one who, like Bagels, was an escape artist. She confesses that she still cries when she watches the movie *Lassie Come Home*. Joan lives in Vancouver, British Columbia, where she writes full-time and teaches part-time. For more information, visit www.joanbettystuchner.blogspot.ca.

ACKNOWLEDGMENTS: I'd like to thank my editor, Amy Collins, as well as all those who told me their dog stories, especially Grace Olson (owner of Wrexford).